Little Red Fox
Stories

MAMMOTH

First published in Great Britain as two separate volumes:

Little Red Fox and the Wicked Uncle
First published by William Heinemann Ltd 1954

Little Red Fox and the Magic Moon
First published by William Heinemann Ltd 1958

This edition published 1992 by Mammoth
an imprint of Reed Consumer Books Ltd
Michelin House, 81 Fulham Road, London SW3 6RB
and Auckland, Melbourne, Singapore and Toronto

Reprinted 1992

Copyright © 1954 and 1958 Alison Uttley and Katherine
Wigglesworth

ISBN 0 7497 0915 4

A CIP catalogue record for this title
is available from the British Library

Printed in Great Britain
by Cox & Wyman Ltd, Reading, Berkshire

Little Red Fox and the Wicked Uncle

Once upon a time there was a little Fox cub. He had no mother and no father, and he was all alone in the wide world of Thorp Wood. Mrs. Badger found the baby Fox crying in a gorse bush one evening. She heard a little sob and then a whimper, so she stopped.

"Here's a babe in the wood," said she.

She put her basket and umbrella on a stone. She pushed aside the yellow gorse flowers and peered at the little Fox. He had bright gold eyes which sparkled in the darkness, and a turned-up nose, and a thick brush of a tail with a white tip, but his red fur was bedraggled and dirty.

"Why don't you go home to your mammy, little Red Fox?" she asked, kindly.

"Haven't got no mammy. Haven't got no home. Haven't got nuffin," wailed the small animal and two fat tears rolled down his snub nose and dropped with a splash on the ground.

Mrs. Badger was upset. She thought of her own happy family.

"I've got two childer of my own," she murmured. "I could make room for another—but a Fox, a bad little Fox! I'm not sure what Mr. Badger would say."

The little Fox looked at her with his golden eyes.

"Haven't had no dinner," said he.

"Will you be good?" asked Mrs. Badger, and he nodded.

"Then I'll try you. Come along with me," said Mrs. Badger, and, picking up her basket and umbrella, she turned away.

The little Red Fox dried his eyes on his tail and ran after her.

That was how the little Red Fox came to live in the Badgers' house, in Thorp Wood, among the rocks and ferns and trees.

Mr. and Mrs. Badger had a nice old house, hidden in the earth with ferns hanging by the door and ivy creeping over the door-posts. There was a stream not far away and a garden where Mr. Badger grew his herbs and vegetables, his pig-nuts and thyme.

As Mrs. Badger and the little Red Fox came near, the door was thrown wide open and Mr. Badger looked out.

"Here you are at last, my dear," said he, taking the heavy basket from his wife.

"Who's that little fellow following after

you?" he continued, staring at the cub.

"A babe in the wood, I found," said Mrs. Badger.

"Had the robins covered him up?" asked Mr. Badger, surprised.

"No, he was in a gorse bush and I want to adopt him," said Mrs. Badger, firmly.

"You know best, my dear," said Mr. Badger, slowly. "You know what Foxes are."

"He's different," said Mrs. Badger, shaking her head to silence her husband. "He's a good little Fox. I can tell by the shape of his nose."

"You know best," said Mr. Badger again. "But he's dirty."

"He'll wash. He won't melt in water," said Mrs. Badger.

"Here's a new brother for you," said Mrs. Badger to her two children who were staring at the wild little animal. She led the Fox indoors and took him to her children.

"Come along, Bonny and Bill. Make room for the Red Fox to sit down. He's come to live with us. His name is Rufus."

Bonny frowned and Bill blinked, but they made room on the seat, and the small Fox squeezed between them. There was a strong foxy smell and they did not like it.

Mrs. Badger put bowls of hot bread and milk on the table, and they gulped it down hungrily. The little Red Fox ate as if he would never have enough.

"It's bath night," said Mrs. Badger and the Fox looked startled. He wondered what a bath was.

Mr. Badger carried in the tub, and poured warm water ready. First Bonny was dipped in it and dried with a big towel. Then Bill had a quick bath. Finally came the turn of the dirty little Fox, and Mr. Badger rubbed him. He soaped him and scoured him, till the tears came to the eyes of the little Red Fox.

"I don't like this," he sobbed, as Mr. Badger pommelled him with his heavy paws. Mrs. Badger poured a bucket of cold water over him, so that he caught his breath and struggled to get away.

When a dripping little miserable Fox sat howling dismally, Mrs. Badger said, "There, he's clean, father. Lift him out." The little Fox scrambled out by himself, upset the tub and dashed for the door.

Mr. Badger caught him, and Mrs. Badger dried him before the fire. As she rubbed she sang a merry little song:—

> "Rub–a–dub–dub,
> Three babes in the tub.
> Bonny and Bill and the little Red Fox,
> All of 'em clean from their heads to
>   their socks.
> All of 'em ready to sleep in the rocks,
> Where nobody never can find 'em."

Mr. Badger played a wheaten whistle, and little Bill and Bonny rapped on the table with wooden spoons. The little Fox was so interested he forgot to cry, and soon he joined in the ditty, shouting "Where nobody never can find 'em."

Mrs. Badger sprinkled some lavender

water over him from a watering-can, and
brushed his hair till it shone red-gold.

"Nobody would know you," said she.
"The huntsmen won't hunt you, the dogs
won't chase you. You are safe from enemies

for we have changed your scent."

She made up a third little bed and the three ran into the tiny stone bedroom cut out of the rocks, with one small green window looking towards the sunrise and another looking towards the sunset.

The little Fox leapt about, rolled over the beds and peeped from a window at the moon.

"The moon's my friend. I knows her," said he, waving a paw.

"He knows the moon," whispered Bonny to Bill.

"Sleep well, Rufus," said Mrs. Badger as

she tucked him up. "We will take care of you."

"I takes care of misself," said the little Red Fox.

That night while the animals slept Mrs. Badger took a piece of blue cloth from her sewing-drawer and made a small coat for the little Red Fox.

"He'll be smart in this," said she, as she sewed on the buttons and put a clean handkerchief in the pocket.

"He's smart enough already," said Mr. Badger, puffing at his pipe. "You mustn't spoil that youngster. Bad Foxes get put in boxes."

Mrs. Badger peeped in the bedroom, and there was the little Fox trying to squeeze through the narrow window.

"What's the matter, Rufus?" she asked, and she grabbed him by the tail.

"Only going to sing to the moon," said he.

"Good Foxes go to sleep. Only naughty Foxes sing to the moon," said Mrs. Badger.

The little Fox winked his sparkling eyes, and got back to bed, and he went to sleep like a lamb.

The next day he awoke early. He stared at his patchwork quilt, and he peeped at the two beds where the little Badgers lay. Up he leapt and tickled their toes.

"Get up. Get up. The sun's dancing," he cried.

Out they all ran to send kisses to the dancing sun and then they washed their faces in the stream, and dried them on dock leaves.

They nibbled a few blades of grass, which is good for all animals.

"Come along, quick," called Mrs. Badger. "Porridge and cream and honeycomb from the wild bees' nest."

Before they sat down Mrs. Badger brought out the blue jacket, and helped the little Fox to get his arms into it. The others watched. They wore pink coats which went well with their striped noses.

The little Fox stroked the blue coat and put his paws in the pockets, but he said nothing.

"Don't you like it?" asked Mrs. Badger, disappointed.

He nodded, and made a ball of the handkerchief.

"When little Badgers get a present they say something," said Mrs. Badger.

"What?" asked the little Fox.

"Thank you, thank you," shouted the two little Badgers.

The little Red Fox suddenly threw his arms about Mrs. Badger.

"I'd rather have a red-green-blue-violet-dandelion-yellow coat, thank you," said he.

"You want the rainbow," said Mrs. Badger, faintly.

They ate their breakfasts, but the little Fox gobbled all and cried, "More. More."

"Please," said Mrs. Badger.

"Please, lots and lots," said the little Fox.

Mr. Badger came in to breakfast. He brought news, but he waited till the three had gone out to play before he spoke.

"There's a great Fox roaming the woods. He's a bad one. He tried to rob the hen-roost last night. He's this little chap's Uncle."

"A wicked Uncle for the babe in the wood," said Mrs. Badger.

"He may try to get the little Fox," continued Mr. Badger.

Mrs. Badger looked out at the three small animals playing leap-frog, and rolling over in furry balls. She beckoned to the little Red Fox, and he danced lightly on his toes.

"Rufus! Beware! There's danger in the woods," said she, solemnly wagging her paw.

The little Red Fox laughed. "I likes danger.

It tastes good," said he, and away he pranced.

The little Red Fox was now one of the family. He played happily with the two Badgers, who thought he was the cleverest brother come to share their home. He could creep like a shadow while they tumbled about. He leapt over walls, while they had to trot round. They went everywhere together, but the little Red Fox was the leader.

They paddled in the stream but he caught the fish by the tails.

They talked to the water-rats but he tickled their noses with a straw. They gazed at the Swan, but he waded out in the river to touch the beautiful feathers.

"Keep away," hissed the Swan, striking him with her beak. "I am no friend of Foxes."

"Why does she do that?" asked the injured little Fox, hurrying back to the shore. "I wouldn't hurt her."

"Swans are princesses in disguise," said Bonny.

21

"Swans can tell fairy tales if they like you,"
said Bill.

"I should like to be friends with her,"
sighed the little Fox, as he watched the ruffled
bird sail proudly away.

Mr. Badger lent the little Fox his wheelbarrow and they all went gardening. Then the little Red Fox had a plan.

"We'll make a grotto for the Swan," said he to his two companions.

They dug up ferns in the wood and planted them by the stream. They made a pool, with

the water falling down the rocks and the ferns hanging over. It was a lovely home for a Swan.

In bed that night the little Red Fox lay
thinking of the snow-white Swan. Would she
come to the pool they had made? There were
forget-me-nots and hart's-tongue ferns, and
rushes growing near.

"I will creep out softly and look," thought
he. "I wish I had a crown for her."

He slipped on his coat and whispered to
Bonny to come with him. She was quieter
than Bill. They went softly through the
kitchen, and the little Red Fox snatched
Mrs. Badger's best hat which hung on a peg.

"She will like this for a crown," said he.

When they crept through the trees to the
pool they saw the white shape of the Swan, a
bird of silver in the moonlight. She was
looking at the water, dipping her beak as if
seeking something.

"Oh lovely Swan," whispered Bonny. "We are so glad you've come. Do be friends with Rufus."

"Please, Princess," added the little Red Fox, "we made this home for you. We've brought you a hat, because we haven't a crown."

The Swan bent her head and the little Fox put the flowery hat upon it. The Swan looked at herself in the water.

"Thank you," said she. "It is very becoming."

"And now will you tell us a story?" asked Bonny.

"About the Princess," added Rufus.

So the Swan graciously began her famous tale.

"Once there was a little Princess who lived in a castle. One day she leaned over the moat, to see herself in the water. Her silver crown fell in, but a lovely Swan caught it as it went deep down, and brought it back to her. So the King gave a little crown to the Swan, and he wore it all his life. He was my great-grandfather. Now the crown is lost, and I am always looking for it, for it is a magic crown."

"Is it in the water?" asked little Bonny, and she began to hunt among the ferns and rushes.

But the little Red Fox, who sat quietly listening to that fluting voice, now gave a shiver. He smelled a queer scent which made his heart beat loudly. He turned and saw a pair of wicked eyes looking from the bushes at the snow-white Swan. It was a great Fox with sharp teeth and a long nose.

The little Red Fox shook with fear but he bravely ran towards this fierce animal.

"Oh, good evening, Uncle Fox," cried he in a loud voice, to warn the Swan. "I hope you are well, Uncle Fox."

The Fox gave a growl of anger and sprang at the Swan, but the little Red Fox who was in

the way, received the blow and fell over. The Swan flapped her wings and slowly flew out of danger, while little Bonny tumbled in the stream.

"What do you mean by making me lose my supper?" cried the Big Fox, crossly, and he cuffed the little Fox and shook him till his teeth rattled and his coat was torn.

"Now you shall come with me. I wanted to catch you," continued the angry Fox, and he dragged Rufus through the woods. After a time he sang in a fusty, rusty voice a song which made the little Red Fox quake.

"Yo-ho! Yo-ho! Yo-ho!
I've got a little Fox,
I'll keep him in a box,
And lock him with a key.
I'll fasten him with wire,
I'll roast him on the fire,
And eat him for my tea."

"Oh, Uncle Fox. You wouldn't do that, would you?" begged the little Red Fox, as he panted and struggled among the briers through which his wicked Uncle pulled him.

"Wouldn't I? You'll see," grunted the Fox.

They reached a tumble-down hut, hidden in a grove of nettles. The Fox swung open the door and threw the little Red Fox inside. Rufus picked himself up and looked about him, at the broken chair, the dying fire, and

the heaps of rags and bones. Oh dear! How he longed for his new mother and the little Badgers!

"I want to go home," said he.

"This is your home," said the Wicked Uncle. "If this isn't good enough for you, I have a better place."

He dragged a sack off a hen-coop and the little Fox saw two poor hens crouching within. He opened the door and pushed the little Fox inside too. There was wire-netting over the front, and the hens and the little Fox were pressed against it.

The Fox fetched a tiny key which hung on a silver loop like a cord of twisted wire, and he locked the door of the coop.

"Uncle! What is that?" asked the little Fox.

"It's the silver crown belonging to the Swan, of course," said the Fox. "I've got the crown and I want her too. I couldn't catch her when she had it on her head."

Then he threw a log on the fire, and made himself a cup of tea. He lighted a candle and began to read a ragged bit of paper. Everything was very quiet. The hens were too frightened to move and the little Fox lay still, pretending to sleep.

After a time the Fox's head nodded, the paper rustled to the floor and snores came squeaking from the Wicked Uncle, snores as loud as the cries of the owl hooting in the wood.

The little Red Fox bided his time. Then he brought from his pocket a bunch of sycamore keys which Bonny had given him. Now the keys of the trees will open any lock when one knows the password, and Father Badger had whispered it to Rufus.

> "Seccamore, seccamore,
>   Please will you loose the door?"

As the little Red Fox murmured these words, the sycamore key (which is the winged fruit of the tree), turned in the lock and the door of

the hen-coop opened. Rufus crept out, and helped the two dazed hens to follow. He took the silver crown with the little key hanging from it and put it on his arm. Then he covered up the hen-coop with the sack and went off in the night.

Away went the three, through the woods, the hens running on their sore toes, flapping their bruised wings. When they reached the farmhouse they fluttered up the narrow hen-stair to their own hen-house.

"Oh, thank you, little Red Fox! We won't forget your kindness. We will lay eggs for you every day."

The little Red Fox galloped home, past the vacant pool, and there he hung the silver crown among the ferns ready for the Swan

when she returned. The sun was rising as he reached home. Mrs. Badger had fallen into an uneasy sleep by the fire, and Mr. Badger was out seeking the lost little Fox.

"The sun is dancing," cried the little Red Fox as he rushed into the house, kissing Mrs. Badger, and tickling the toes of sleepy Bill and Bonny.

"Oh, Rufus! We thought we had lost you for ever," cried Mrs. Badger, hugging him.

"Oh, Rufus! How did you escape from your Wicked Uncle?" cried Bonny, springing from her bed with Bill running after her.

"Was danger nice?" asked Bill.

"Not so bad," answered the little Red Fox. "Danger tore my coat, but I got away and two hens escaped with me, and I found the silver crown belonging to the Swan."

"Oh, Rufus!" they exclaimed, admiringly.

"It hangs by the pool, ready for the Swan," said he.

So Mrs. Badger made a feast for breakfast, with pies and bacon, with jellies and doughnuts and everything she could find in the larder. When Mr. Badger came home, weary with his search, there they all sat, laughing and singing the song of the Wicked Uncle, which Rufus was teaching them.

"Yo-ho! Yo-ho! Yo-ho!
I've got a little Fox,
I'll keep him in a box,
And lock him with a key.
I'll fasten him with wire,
I'll roast him on the fire,
And eat him for my tea."

Mr. Badger looked at the turned-up nose of the little Red Fox.

"You are right, my dear," said he to his wife.

As for the Wicked Uncle, he never noticed that the hen-coop was empty till the next morning, when he went to cook the hens for breakfast, and to make the little Red Fox do all the work.

"I'll catch you the next time," he cried, and he shook his hairy fist and danced with rage.

Little Red Fox and
the Magic Moon

One day the sun shone so hard that spickles and sparkles flashed on the beech leaves, and every blade of grass was like a silver fish. The sun laughed when the little Red Fox leapt lightly on his toes, and it sent golden rays to warm the small fox's fur.

Mrs. Badger came to the door of the stone cottage under the hill. She waved her apron like a flag, and then she banged two stones together, to call her family to dinner.

"Clack! Clack! Clack!" went the stones. "Dinner. Dinner," they seemed to say.

Bill and Bonny came hurrying from the wood where they had been digging for treasure. The little Red Fox danced over the bars of light and shadow and ran into the house. He looked at the table and he sighed deeply, but Bonny and Bill cried "Dinner, Dinner!" as they ran through the doorway.

41

They sat at the table grasping their wooden spoons, but the little Red Fox tied a string made of grasses to his spoon and pretended it was a fishing-rod.

"Come, eat your dinner, Rufus," said Mrs. Badger, stirring his bowl of soup.

"I'm tired of herb pudding and nettle soup.

I don't like what-we-have," pouted the little Red Fox.

Bill and Bonny stared at their foster-brother. What was the matter? They liked good green nettle soup, and they loved herb pudding with marjoram and elderflowers and wild thyme.

"Eat your dinner, Rufus," said Mrs. Badger, patiently.

"I'm going fishing, Mammy Badger," said the little Red Fox looking up at her with a foxy smile, and waving his spoon. "I'll make a fishing-rod and go fishing in the river and catch lots of fish for you to fry for dinner."

"That you won't," said Mrs. Badger. His bright smile faded, but he tried again.

"I wants to go fishing, please, Mammy Badger. I loves you, I do," said the little Red

Fox, and he threw her a kiss.

"You would get drowned dead for sure. You'd fall in. I can't lose my bad little Fox," said Mrs. Badger, patting his head.

"I can swim," said the little Red Fox, proudly.

"You'd meet a man or a foxhound, or a crocodile," said Mrs. Badger.

"A croc — — crocodile?" cried the little Red Fox. "How exciting!"

"He likes danger," chimed in the little Badgers admiringly. "Let's all go fishing, Mammy."

"Eat your dinners," said Mrs. Badger, but as they ate their herb pudding and drank the fresh spring water she changed her mind. She looked at the sky and smelled at the wind.

"You shall go," she said. "When the wind's in the south, it blows bait into the fishes' mouths. I should like a nice fat trout for your father's supper."

"Oh, thank you, Mammy Badger," they cried, hugging her. They cut willow branches and tied wriggling worms to the ends for bait. The little Red Fox knew exactly how to make a fishing-rod.

Then they wove a rush basket to carry the fish, and lined it with fresh grass. They ran down the field and across the wood to the

river bank. They sat in a row, three little animals each with a slender rod and wriggling worm dangling over the water.

"Keep very quiet, Bonny. Don't speak, Bill," whispered the little Red Fox. "Those fish mustn't know we are here."

The sun beat down, making every wave flash and twinkle, so that it looked like

thousands of glittering gold fish. Down below, in the cool dark water every little fish laughed at the three shadows above them.

"Little Red Fox goes fishing," chanted the fish. "Little Bill and Bonny Badger goes fishing too. Won't catch us."

They flirted their tails and set free the little worms, and then they put water weeds on the hooks.

"They're biting," whispered the little Red Fox, excitedly.

But the fish leapt high in the air, right under the noses of the three and they turned

46

somersaults as they dropped back into the river.

"Lots of fish, all flying," said the little Red Fox. "I'll sing to them and enchant them."

He made a dish of dock leaves and held it ready. Then in a squeaky voice he sang to them.

> "Pretty little fishy,
> Come to my dishy,
> And we'll all have tea."

For a minute there was only the ripple of water and then many small voices sweet as bells came to the astonished animals.

"We have no wishy
To leap on a dishy,
For nobody's tea."

"Did you hear that?" exclaimed Bonny. They all kept very still and from the river came a chorus of many fishes.

"We lives in the water,
So you didn't oughter
Catch fishes for your tea."

"Did you hear that?" asked Bill.

"Yes," said the little Red Fox, slowly. "P'raps we didn't oughter catch fishes for our tea."

They picked up their fishing-rods, but down the river came the snow-white Swan, gliding along in her beauty. On her head she wore the little silver crown, and her feathers were curved like sails, as she moved on the glittering water.

"Little Red Fox? What are you doing? Fishing?" she asked in her soft voice which hardly anyone hears. "You can't catch these fish, you know."

"Why not?" asked the little Red Fox.

"Because they are too clever to be caught," replied the Swan. "They all go to school, down in the river, and they learn about Foxes and Badgers and Man. Come here in the evening. Then you will see many things. The moon will be full and you can catch some moonshine, or a star maybe."

They stayed on the river bank, watching
the Swan, listening to the water, looking at
the busy water-rats at their house doors, and
the dippers hopping from stone to stone, and
the kingfishers flying with emerald wings, the

pied wagtails shaking their long tails and the willow-warblers singing down the scale.

"There's Peggy Whitethroat and Peggy

Dishwasher," said the little Red Fox. "I knows them all. Hello, Peggy," and he waved his paw to the willow-warblers and the wagtails.

"They've come to do their washing," he explained.

On the way home they filled their basket with mushrooms and crab-apples and berries.

"Didn't catch any fish," said little Red Fox to Mrs. Badger. "They didn't want to be caught. They sang to us."

"Fishes are artful," said Mr. Badger, slowly sucking his pipe.

"Tell us about them," said Bonny.

So after supper Mr. Badger sat in the doorway and told his family about all the creatures of the river, the little fish, and the big salmon, the lively beautiful trout, the elvers who come to live there, the lowly caddis worms and the water-boatmen who skate on the surface of shallows.

"Do starfish and moonfish live in the river?" asked Rufus.

"Starfish live in the sea, and I don't know about moonfish," said Mr. Badger. "You'd best get off to bed and dream about them."

But the little Red Fox didn't go to sleep. He

waited till Bonny and Bill were snoring and then he leapt from his bed, slipped on his jacket, opened the window wide and skipped into the moonlight.

"Hello, Mrs. Moon," said he, making a deep bow to the lovely moon, and the moon bowed back to the little Red Fox.

"I might catch a moonfish for Mammy Badger," thought the little Red Fox, as he grabbed his fishing-rod from the bush where he had left it.

He arrived safely at the river, although there were some queer little noises of owls and weasels on the way. Down there everything was different and much more exciting. He raised his nose and sniffed at the scents of

the river bank. There was a strong smell of wet mud which was delicious, and the fragrance of water-mint and wild geranium and meadow-sweet, and the rich odour of moss and leaves.

The river was alive, it sang very loudly indeed as it rushed over the rocks, with foaming flecks of white and silky little water-falls. In the waves were broken gold stars and a crooked gold moon which shone like the stars and moon in the sky above.

"Two moons," said the little Red Fox under his breath. "Lots of starfish."

He threw his line into the water and at once caught a scrap of moonshine. He put it in his pocket. Then he fished again, and a little gold star came out.

He placed it on the grass, where it lay thin and watery, shining with a light of its own. He fished again and caught another and soon he had a pile of gold.

The white Swan came silently down the river, and she stayed near, paddling with her brown feet against the swift water. The little Fox did not see her, he was so intent on his fishing.

"Haven't you caught enough, little Red

Fox? You can't carry all that starlight home. You will rob the river."

"Oh, you frightened me," cried the little Fox. "Does it matter, fishing up all these stars?"

"One's enough," said the Swan. "Throw the rest back, little Red Fox."

The little Fox hesitated a moment and then he tossed the stars into the river, where white hands seemed to stretch up and catch them.

"Who are those?" stammered the little Fox.

"The water-nymphs who live here," answered the Swan.

As the little Red Fox stood staring, trying

to see the water-nymphs, a small boat came down the river. It rested against a rock, and the river gently tossed it up and down.

"Look! Look! A boat," he cried, excitedly. He dived into the river and swam boldly to the tiny craft. He scrambled in without upsetting her, and found two oars.

"She's a runaway boat," said the Swan. "She once belonged to the Otters, but they didn't want her, so away she went. I saw her a few days ago, caught in the reeds, but she has got free."

"Can I have her?" asked the little Red Fox.

"Yes," answered the Swan. "Yes, if you're good."

"Thank you, Lady Swan," replied the little Red Fox, and he rowed to the bank and tied the painter to a tree. He washed the boat with a bunch of leaves and baled out the water, and shook the damp cushions. She was a very small boat, ruddy as a chestnut, and her name was painted on the side. The little Red Fox was not good at reading, but he knew the name was *Water-lily* because there was a picture of a water-lily for all to see.

"Good-bye, little Red Fox. Good-bye, Water-lily," said the Swan, and she drifted on her way, swimming slowly with the river on a pale band of moonshine.

"I'll hide her so that nobody can find her," thought the little Red Fox, and he dragged the boat up the bank, untying the rope and stowing the oars. She came so easily he found he could lift her by himself.

"I'll carry her home to Mammy Badger," said he.

He tilted the boat on his back and walked on all fours, with his small legs just appearing underneath, so that he looked like a tortoise waddling along under its shell. He couldn't see where he was going, and the boat seemed to grow heavier, as all things get heavy on a long walk. He wished he had Bonny and Bill

to help him, and he wished he could see the moon.

Suddenly the boat was pushed hard over him, and he sank to the ground, completely smothered. The boat was tight upon his back like a shell on a nut.

"I'm caught. I'm in a trap," he thought in a panic. He dare not shout for help. There was a loud chuckle from the bottom of the boat, as somebody thumped on the wood. Then a rough barking voice began to sing a hateful song which the little Red Fox had heard before.

60

"Yo-ho! Yo-ho! Yo-ho!
I've got a Little Fox . . .
    or crocodile.
I'll keep him in a box . . .
    for just-a-while.
I'll cook him with some herbs . . .
    and camomile."

The little Red Fox knew it was his wicked uncle the Big Fox from the woods. There was no escape at all, unless of course the Fox thought he really was a crocodile. "I likes danger," whispered the little Fox, but a tear trickled down his nose. "I likes danger when Mammy Badger is near, not all by myself in a big wood with a Fox on top of me."

With difficulty he put his paw in his pocket to get his handkerchief, and he brought out the bit of moonshine, like a silver scarf. It shone in the boat and cheered him. Then he brought out the prickly star. It gleamed like a lamp in the darkness. He could see the red cushion which was squeezed on his head, and the oars tucked into the side of the boat, and the end of the Fox's brush which poked underneath. He longed to give it a tug but dare not touch it, although it tickled his face.

"Yo–ho there! Yo–ho there!" called the Big Fox, listening, and the little Red Fox scarcely breathed.

"Is it my nephew Rufus, or is it somebody else?" called the Fox, who was puzzled by the silence.

"Ug–ug–ug–ug," growled the little Red Fox, trying to be a crocodile.

"Hum," murmured the puzzled Fox. "Surely I didn't make a mistake? Surely I caught my nephew the little Red Fox? Surely it isn't a great brown crocodile?"

"Is it you, Rufus?" he asked again.

"Ug–ug–ug–ug," roared Rufus under the boat. His voice echoed in the roof above him; it rumbled and growled under the Big Fox. Then the little Red Fox gave a nip at the Big Fox's brush.

"I'll soon find out who is under this boat," said the Fox fiercely, and he sprang down and raised the bow. He only lifted it a crack lest whatever was underneath should escape.

The little Red Fox flashed the bright star in his eyes and fluttered the silver moonbeams over him, so that he leapt back in alarm and sat on the boat again.

"I've caught something, and it may be something to eat, and then again, it may be something that will eat me," he thought. He sniffed, but the boat smelled of river mud and tar. He listened but there was never a sound. He tried to peer through the boat, but the seams were close, and only a bright light shone where the rowlocks touched the grass, for the little Fox kept the star in his hand and flashed it around.

Now up in the sky the moon was looking at this scene in the woods where a Big Fox sat on top of a little boat, and a sparkle came now and then like a heavenly light.

"There's one of my river stars, and some of my own moonshine," said the moon to Venus, who also was shining up there. "The star is under a boat. It wants help. It is signalling. Some wild creature is held down by that cruel Fox. I'll send an earth creature to the rescue, and who is better than that old Badger, lumbering along there?"

The moon flashed down her light, she shot her own moonbeams on the Big Fox, so that

he quivered. They were like silver arrows piercing his fur, and he looked so bright that Mr. Badger came to see what was the matter.

"What are you hiding there?" asked the Badger.

"I don't know what it is," said the Fox, sliding off the boat. "You can keep it. It may be a crocodile, and it may be a lion, escaped. Be careful, Badger."

The Fox slipped among the trees. "I wonder what that creature was!" he muttered. "He walked like my nephew Rufus, he had the same little legs, but he was strong enough to carry that boat and he roared mightily."

Mr. Badger cautiously lifted the boat, and out crept the little Red Fox, with a star in one paw and a scarf of moonshine in another paw.

"Oh, Daddy Badger, I am glad you've come," cried the little Fox. He threw his arms round his foster-father's legs and hugged him with moonlight and star.

"So it's you, Rufus," grunted the Badger. "I thought you were fast asleep in bed, you naughty little Fox."

"But how did you know I was here?" asked the little Red Fox.

"I didn't know. I just comed to see what the moon was shining on. The moon led me here," said the Badger.

"The moon's my friend," said the little Red Fox.

Then the moon, who saw the little Red Fox with the star in his paw and the wisp of moonshine on his shoulder, pulled a cloud over her face.

"So it was the little Red Fox who was caught," said she. "I am the friend of little Foxes and Badgers and little Otters and all night creatures who get lost or frightened."

"Where did this boat come from?" asked Father Badger, turning the little boat over and staring at her graceful shape.

"The Swan gave her to me, for all of us," said the little Red Fox. "I was taking her home when my uncle caught me."

"And this bright star, and this bit of moonshine?" asked the Badger.

"I fished them out of the river," confessed the little Red Fox.

"A bit of moonshine and a star may come

in useful," said the Badger, thoughtfully. "Now we'll go home before your mother misses you," he added.

"Yes, Daddy Badger," said the little Fox meekly. He was so sleepy now he could hardly keep his eyes open.

They trudged home, the little Red Fox following his foster-father who carried the boat. Everyone was asleep, and the tired Fox crept into bed and he, too, fell asleep at once. Mr. Badger put the boat in the house for safety. Then he picked up the star and moon-shine which lay on the floor. They shone so brightly he stood for a minute looking at them.

"They ought to be in water," he muttered. "Very funny things are these re-flections. Yes, re-flections, that's what they are."

So he dropped them into a bucket of water, where Bill Badger and Bonny found them the next morning, shining with light.

"Look at this star, and a shiny bit of a moon, swimming in the water-bucket," they cried. "Have they come out of the sky?"

They stooped and tried to pick them up, but it was impossible. The star and the moon-light trickled through their paws and danced on the ruffled water surface.

Then they saw the boat under the table.

"Oh! Oh! A boat! *The Water-lily*," cried Bonny stroking the painted flower.

"Where has she come from?" asked Bill.

Mr. Badger came in from the garden, for he had been out to watch the sun rise and to welcome the new day. Mrs. Badger came running in with a couple of eggs.

"It's a present, given to young Rufus," said Mr. Badger. "He's been out fishing by night, and he was cotched by that great old Fox and shut under this boat."

"That's why he's so tired this morning,"

said Mrs. Badger, and she put the eggs in a saucepan. "He's fast asleep."

"He likes danger, Mammy," said Bonny.

"He got it this time," said Mr. Badger.

"What did I get?" asked the little Fox leaping into the room.

"Oh, Rufus. You've waked up," cried Bonny.

"You got a boat, from somewhere," said Bill, sternly.

"Yes, it's my boat, given me by the Swan. We are all going out in it, if there's room," said the little Red Fox, and he seized Bill and Bonny unaware and pushed them backward

into the boat, so that eight little stiff legs waggled in the air.

"Come! Come!" said Mrs. Badger. "Don't be rough, Rufus. Here's some honeycomb your father found last night in a hollow tree."

"I like what–we–have to–day," said the little Red Fox. "I like honeycomb. Is that why you were out in the woods, Daddy Badger?"

"Yes. I'm glad I went after that honeycomb, for you were fairly cotched by that great ole Fox, and he would have taken you to his den," said Mr. Badger.

"And made you wash up and cook and scrub for him," added Bonny, scrambling from the boat.

"And serve you right," said Bill.

They ate their honey breakfast, and made plans for a picnic away up the river, that very same day.

"Honey and new bread and fresh butter," said Mrs. Badger. "While you children ride on the water, your father and I will sit on the

bank ready to rescue you when you fall in."

"We won't go fishing there," said Rufus, "but we shall see a water-nymph with a gold star, and we'll talk to Peggy Whitethroat and

Peggy Dishwasher, and the kingfishers, and the tall herons, and perhaps we shall see a crocodile."

Then he noticed the bucket of water with the shining star and the scrap of moonshine.

"Can we keep these, Daddy Badger?" he asked.

"Yes," said the old Badger. "I shall put the bucket in the dark passage, and then there will always be a light for us."

"Just like the moon and a star shining there," said the little Red Fox. "Even when there's no moon in the sky, we shall have one of our very own."

He munched his bread and honeycomb and murmured: "The moon's my friend. I caught a bit of her scarf when I went fishing and she's given it to me to keep."

Also by Alison Uttley

MORE LITTLE RED FOX STORIES

The mischievous Little Red Fox and the Good Little Badgers go to the Fair and have a real adventure when they rescue the Little White Rabbit from the Big Bad Fox. Little Red Fox also discovers a baby unicorn who eventually helps Rufus face his Wicked Uncle . . .

Patricia Coombs

DORRIE AND THE GOBLIN

'A little Goblin is BIG TROUBLE!'

When a basket is left at the back door, Dorrie is amazed by the little furry red-eyed creature inside. The Cook and her mother, the Big Witch, are horrified – but Dorrie is determined to look after the Goblin. However, she soon discovers that even a very small Goblin can cause an *awful* lot of trouble!

A delightful, funny story for beginning readers about Dorrie and her cat Gink. There are other stories with Dorrie and Gink to enjoy in:

> *Dorrie and the Birthday Eggs*
> *Dorrie and the Haunted House*
> *Dorrie and the Wizard's Spell*

W. J. Corbett

THE BEAR WHO STOOD ON HIS HEAD

Ben the bear is as round as a butterball and his eyes are the colour of chewed toffee. He is the baby bear of the family. But wherever he goes, disaster follows! His sister and brother are fed up with him spoiling their adventures and get very angry. But when Ben gets upset, he stands on his head and weeps until tears trickle into his ears . . .

Ben the roly-poly bear is simply irresistible!

By the winner of the Whitbread Award.

Jill Tomlinson

THE OWL WHO WAS AFRAID OF THE DARK

Plop is exactly the same as every baby barn owl that has ever been – except for one thing. Plop is afraid of the dark. His parents keep telling him that dark is best, but it's no use. Plop just wants to be a day bird. Finally, his mother pushes him out of the nest to ask other people what *they* think of the dark, and Plop is amazed at their replies . . .

The best-known of Jill Tomlinson's popular books, *The Owl Who Was Afraid of the Dark* has become a modern classic. There are lots more animals to meet in this delightful series –

The Aardvark Who Wasn't Sure
The Cat Who Wanted to Go Home
The Gorilla Who Wanted to Grow Up
The Hen Who Wouldn't Give Up
The Otter Who Wanted to Know
Penguin's Progress

A selected list of titles available from Mammoth

While every effort is made to keep prices low, it is sometimes necessary to increase prices at short notice. Mandarin Paperbacks reserves the right to show new retail prices on covers which may differ from those previously advertised in the text or elsewhere.

The prices shown below were correct at the time of going to press.

☐	7497 0366 0	**Dilly the Dinosaur**	Tony Bradman	£2.50
☐	7497 0137 4	**Flat Stanley**	Jeff Brown	£2.50
☐	7497 0306 7	**The Chocolate Touch**	P Skene Catling	£2.50
☐	7497 0568 X	**Dorrie and the Goblin**	Patricia Coombs	£2.50
☐	7497 0114 5	**Dear Grumble**	W J Corbett	£2.50
☐	7497 0054 8	**My Naughty Little Sister**	Dorothy Edwards	£2.50
☐	7497 0723 2	**The Little Prince (colour ed.)**	A Saint-Exupery	£3.99
☐	7497 0305 9	**Bill's New Frock**	Anne Fine	£2.99
☐	7497 0590 6	**Wild Robert**	Diana Wynne Jones	£2.50
☐	7497 0661 9	**The Six Bullerby Children**	Astrid Lindgren	£2.50
☐	7497 0319 9	**Dr Monsoon Taggert's Amazing Finishing Academy**	Andrew Matthews	£2.50
☐	7497 0420 9	**I Don't Want To!**	Bel Mooney	£2.50
☐	7497 0833 6	**Melanie and the Night Animal**	Gillian Rubinstein	£2.50
☐	7497 0264 8	**Akimbo and the Elephants**	A McCall Smith	£2.50
☐	7497 0048 3	**Friends and Brothers**	Dick King-Smith	£2.50
☐	7497 0795 X	**Owl Who Was Afraid of the Dark**	Jill Tomlinson	£2.99

All these books are available at your bookshop or newsagent, or can be ordered direct from the publisher. Just tick the titles you want and fill in the form below.

Mandarin Paperbacks, Cash Sales Department, PO Box 11, Falmouth, Cornwall TR10 9EN.

Please send cheque or postal order, no currency, for purchase price quoted and allow the following for postage and packing:

UK including BFPO   £1.00 for the first book, 50p for the second and 30p for each additional book ordered to a maximum charge of £3.00.

Overseas including Eire   £2 for the first book, £1.00 for the second and 50p for each additional book thereafter.

NAME (Block letters) ....

ADDRESS ....

....

☐ I enclose my remittance for ....

☐ I wish to pay by Access/Visa Card Number

Expiry Date